THE LOST
LETTERS OF CHRISTMAS

WRITTEN BY

LISA RENÉE RUGGERI

1

To my parents, for always bringing the magic to Christmas...

4

CHAPTER 1

WELCOME TO
BRAMBLEWOOD

Sadie's heart sank a little deeper in her chest as the car came to a stop in front of the house. She felt a heavy lump settle in her stomach. *Home*, she thought, but it didn't feel like home. It felt like a place out of a ghost story, like the kind of house that might creak and groan at night, whispering secrets to those brave enough to listen.

"It's perfect, don't you think?" her mother said, trying to sound cheerful, though her voice was strained and tired. Her dad was already out of the car, talking excitedly about all the space they would have. Sadie nodded, but her smile was small and tight. She felt a sharp sting in her chest, a longing ache for the friends and family she'd left behind. Christmas was only weeks away, but it felt like a distant star, barely visible in a dark and lonely sky.

Dragging her feet, Sadie followed her parents up the cracked stone path. The air was cold and sharp, nipping at her cheeks like tiny teeth. She pulled her scarf tighter around her neck, wishing it could wrap all the way around her heart.

Inside, the house was no better. The hallway stretched out in front of her, dim and dusty, with floors that groaned under the weight of her steps. The wallpaper was faded, peeling at the edges like the pages of an old, forgotten book. Cobwebs hung like delicate lace in the corners of the ceiling, and the air smelled faintly of damp wood and something old, something that felt like memories she didn't belong to.

Sadie's parents were already bustling about, their voices echoing through the empty rooms as they talked about where the furniture would go and how they would decorate. Sadie only half-listened. She drifted toward a window, peeking out to see the town beyond – small and still, with only a few people hurriedly moving through the streets, bundled up against the cold. A few children were playing in the snow, their laughter muffled by the wind. She watched them for a moment, feeling a sharp twist of longing in her chest. She imagined her old friends back home, probably hanging up Christmas decorations and planning their holiday parties.

It won't be the same this year, she thought, swallowing back the lump in her throat. *It just won't be the same.*

Upstairs, she found her new room at the end of a long, narrow hallway. The door creaked loudly as she pushed it open, and the room itself was small and square, with a window that overlooked the backyard. The walls were painted a dull shade of yellow that seemed to hold on to the shadows, making the room feel darker and smaller than it was. A single, lonely bed sat in the corner, its frame old and wooden, and a wardrobe stood against the opposite wall, its doors slightly ajar, like it might be hiding a secret.

Sadie sat on the edge of her bed, the mattress creaking beneath her. She pulled her knees to her chest and stared at the floor, where a small, worn rug lay, its vibrancy faded like everything else in this house. She sighed, a deep, heavy sigh that seemed to come from the very core of her heart. December 1st, and not a speck of Christmas spirit to be found. She glanced at the window, where snowflakes began to drift down from the sky, light and soft like feathers. They tapped against the glass, as if trying to say hello, but Sadie turned away. Her chest felt tight, like a band squeezing around her heart, and she felt tears prick at the corners of her eyes. She didn't want to cry - not on the first day in a new town, in a new house. But she felt so far away from everything she loved, like a ship lost at sea with no land in sight.

"Why did we have to move?" she whispered, hugging her knees tighter. "Why now? Right before Christmas?"

But there was no answer, only the soft whisper of the wind outside and the distant creaking of the house as if it were settling into its own sadness. Sadie felt a shiver run down her spine, not from the cold, but from the emptiness that seemed to echo all around her. She missed her friends, she missed her old home, and she missed the way Christmas used to feel – warm and bright, full of laughter and love.

She closed her eyes and tried to imagine the twinkling lights on the tree back home, the smell of freshly baked cookies, and the sound of carol singers on the street corner. But when she opened them again, all she saw was the dim, dusty room and the snow falling silently outside.

Sadie took a deep breath and whispered to herself, "Maybe this house has some magic after all... I just have to find it." But even as she said the words, she felt a flicker of doubt. Was there any magic left to find?

She lay back on the bed, listening to the creaks and groans of the old house, and wondered what secrets it might be hiding. Little did she know, beneath the floorboards, a mystery was waiting to be discovered – one that would change her Christmas forever.

Chapter 2

The First Day

The next morning, Sadie awoke to the sound of clattering dishes and the low hum of conversation drifting up from the kitchen. She blinked in the dim light, momentarily confused about where she was, until the peeling yellow wallpaper and the chill in the air reminded her. *Bramblewood. The new house.* Sadie sighed, feeling that heavy weight settle back in her chest.

She pushed off the thin blanket and rubbed her eyes, then shivered as her feet hit the cold wooden floor. From the window, she could see that a fresh layer of snow had blanketed the ground overnight, covering everything in a soft, glistening white. It looked beautiful, like a postcard scene from some faraway winter wonderland. But to Sadie, it only made everything feel even quieter, even more unfamiliar.

She trudged down the stairs, her feet dragging with every step. As she entered the kitchen, she saw her mum at the stove, hurriedly flipping pancakes while balancing a phone between her shoulder and ear. Her dad was sitting at the small kitchen table, surrounded by piles of papers, his brow furrowed as he typed furiously on his laptop.

"Morning, sweetie!" her mum said, managing a quick smile before turning her attention back to the pancakes. "Did you sleep well?"

Sadie shrugged. "It was okay." She glanced at the empty walls of the kitchen and then back at her mum. "When are we going to decorate for Christmas?"

Her mum's smile faltered for just a second, and she exchanged a quick look with Sadie's dad. "Oh, well... I know we're a bit late this year," she said, trying to sound cheerful. "But things have just been so busy with the move, and both of us starting new jobs... We haven't even unpacked all the boxes yet!" She let out a small, nervous laugh.

"But it's December 2nd already," Sadie pressed. "Back home, we always had the tree up by now. And lights on the porch, and the wreath on the door..."

"I know, honey," her dad interrupted gently, looking up from his laptop. "But this year is different, remember? A lot of changes, and we're still settling in. Maybe... maybe you could help us out with the decorations this time?"

Sadie felt her heart sink a little further. "Me?" she echoed, feeling a little lost. "But... it's a family thing. We're supposed to do it together."

Her dad smiled softly. "I know, Sadie, and we will. It just might not be right away. Maybe you could start by unpacking some of the boxes and seeing what you can find? We'll join in as soon as we can, promise."

Her mum nodded, flipping another pancake. "That's right, sweetie. We're just trying to get through this busy patch. We know it's not the same, but you're so creative! I bet you'll make the house look magical in no time."

Sadie bit her lip, feeling a lump form in her throat. It didn't feel right. It didn't feel fair. Christmas was supposed to be special, something they all did together. Now, it seemed like it was just one more thing she had to do on her own.

"Okay," she mumbled, not wanting to argue. "I'll try."

"Thank you, sweetheart," her dad said with a soft smile. "We really appreciate it. We'll make time, I promise. Just give us a little more time to get settled."

Sadie nodded, but inside she felt a storm brewing. She quickly grabbed a pancake and slathered it with syrup, hoping the sweetness would help swallow down the bitterness she felt creeping in. She ate in silence, listening to the sounds of her parents' busy chatter, their voices distant and hurried. She felt invisible, like a ghost drifting through their busy world.

Later that morning, with her backpack slung over one shoulder, Sadie found herself standing at the end of the driveway, staring down the road. Her breath puffed out in little white clouds, and her hands were stuffed deep into her coat pockets. She was waiting for the school bus, feeling a nervous flutter in her stomach. Her first day at a new school. A school where she knew no one.

She looked back at the house, where her mum and dad were still busy moving around, their shadows flickering behind the frosted windows. They had given her a quick hug, a rushed goodbye, and now here she was, alone again. She let out a slow breath, trying to steady herself.

The bus arrived with a loud, rattling noise, its brakes squealing as it came to a stop. The doors swung open with a loud creak, and Sadie hesitated for a moment before climbing aboard. Inside, the air was warm but filled with a dull hum of chatter, and every eye seemed to turn toward her as she stepped inside. She could feel her cheeks flush with heat as she made her way down the narrow aisle, searching for an empty seat.

Finally, she spotted a seat near the back, next to a girl with curly brown hair and glasses. Sadie slid in beside her, offering a small smile, but the girl barely looked up, her nose buried in a book. Sadie sighed softly and turned to look out the window, watching the town pass by in a blur of white and grey.

The bus ride felt like an eternity, every bump and jolt adding to the knot of nerves in her stomach. By the time they reached the school, her hands were clenched tightly in her lap, her heart pounding in her chest. She followed the crowd of kids into the building, feeling small and out of place.

Inside, the halls were narrow and dimly lit, with walls painted a dull beige. It smelled faintly of old books and floor polish. Sadie glanced around, trying to get her bearings, but the sea of unfamiliar faces made her feel dizzy. She clutched her backpack strap tighter, feeling lost in a wave of noise and movement.

Just then, a stern voice cut through the air. "You must be the new girl," it said.

Sadie turned to see a tall woman standing by the door, her blonde hair pulled back into a tight bun, her lips pressed into a thin line. Her eyes were crystal blue but sharp and cold, like little bits of ice. Sadie felt a shiver run down her spine.

"I'm Miss Jeffers," the woman said, her voice clipped and no-nonsense. "Your teacher."

Sadie swallowed hard and nodded. "Yes, ma'am," she mumbled.

Miss Jeffers raised an eyebrow. "Speak up, dear. I don't have time to strain my ears. You're Sadie, correct?"

"Yes, ma'am," Sadie repeated, a little louder this time. "Sadie Miller."

"Well, Sadie Miller, we don't tolerate tardiness here. I expect you to be on time from now on." Miss Jeffers didn't even wait for Sadie to respond before she turned on her heel and marched down the hallway. "Follow me," she commanded over her shoulder.

Sadie hurried to keep up, her heart racing. She had never met a teacher like this before. Her old teacher, Mrs. Carmichael, had been warm and kind, always wearing a bright smile. Miss Jeffers seemed like the complete opposite – like a storm cloud ready to burst.

They arrived at a classroom with a large wooden door that looked as old as the school itself. Miss Jeffers pushed it open, revealing a room filled with rows of desks, all facing a large blackboard covered in neat chalk writing. The other students were already seated, their eyes turning to Sadie as she stepped inside. She felt their stares like tiny pinpricks on her skin.

"Class, this is Sadie Miller," Miss Jeffers announced without much enthusiasm. "She's new here. Make her feel... welcomed." There was a slight pause before the word "welcomed," as if Miss Jeffers had to force it out of her mouth.

Sadie felt her cheeks grow warm again as a few murmurs rippled through the room. Miss Jeffers pointed to an empty desk near the front. "You'll sit there," she said. "And no talking unless I call on you."

Sadie nodded quickly and made her way to the desk, her heart pounding in her chest. She slid into the seat and tried to make herself as small as possible, hoping the floor might just open up and swallow her whole.

The morning dragged on slowly, with Miss Jeffers's voice droning on and on, like a monotone buzz that filled the room. Sadie tried to pay attention, but her mind kept wandering. She wondered if her friends back home were thinking about her, if they missed her as much as she missed them. She thought about Christmas, and how different it would be this year. She wondered if there was any way to make it feel right again.

At lunch, Sadie found herself standing in the cafeteria with a tray of food, looking for a place to sit. The room was loud and bustling, filled with the sounds of laughter and chatter. She scanned the tables, feeling that familiar knot in her stomach, until she spotted the girl from the bus – the one with the curly hair and glasses. She was sitting alone, reading a book while picking at her lunch.

Sadie took a deep breath and made her way over. "Hi," she said, trying to sound friendly. "Can I sit here?"

The girl looked up, her eyes widening slightly behind her glasses. "Oh, um... sure," she said, scooting over to make room. "I'm Emma."

"Sadie," she replied, setting her tray down. "I'm new here."

"I know," Emma said with a small smile. "Everyone knows. Bramblewood isn't exactly a big place."

Sadie managed a small laugh. "Yeah, I guess not." She glanced around the cafeteria. "What's it like here?"

Emma shrugged. "It's okay, I guess. Not much ever happens. Miss Jeffers is... well, you've met her. She's pretty strict."

Sadie nodded. "She seems... kind of scary."

Emma's smile widened a bit. "She is. Most kids say she's like the Grinch who stole Christmas. But worse."

Sadie giggled, feeling a little lighter. "Yeah, I got that impression."

They chatted for a while, and Sadie found herself relaxing a bit. Emma seemed nice, and even though she was a little shy, she was easy to talk to. Sadie started to feel a tiny spark of hope. Maybe, just maybe, things wouldn't be so bad after all.

But as the afternoon wore on, the day dragged on slowly, and Sadie found herself counting the minutes until the final bell rang. By the time it did, she felt exhausted, like she had been holding her breath all day. She gathered her things and headed toward the door, hoping to catch the bus home.

Just as she reached the door, Miss Jeffers called out, "Sadie! A moment, please."

Sadie froze and turned slowly, her stomach tightening. "Yes, ma'am?" she said, her voice barely above a whisper.

Miss Jeffers looked at her with those cold, sharp eyes. "I expect better from you, young lady. You seemed distracted today, and I do not tolerate distraction in my classroom."

"I... I'm sorry," Sadie stammered. "I'll try harder."

Miss Jeffers gave a curt nod. "See that you do. Dismissed."

Sadie hurried out of the room, her face burning with embarrassment. As she stepped outside, the cold air hit her like a slap, and she took a deep breath, trying to shake off the feeling of dread that had settled in her chest.

She made her way to the bus stop, her steps slow and heavy. The snow was falling again, thick and soft, blanketing the world in white. She looked up at the sky, watching the snowflakes drift down, and whispered, "Please... let there be some magic here. Somewhere."

And though the wind carried her words away, Sadie couldn't help but feel a flicker of hope, small and fragile, like a candle in the dark. Maybe tomorrow would be better. Maybe, somewhere in this strange new town, there was still a bit of magic left to find.

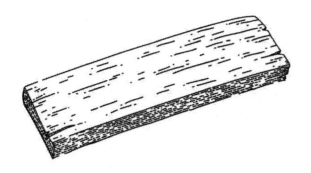

Chapter 3

The Squeaky Floorboards

That evening, after the long and exhausting day at school, Sadie dragged herself up the creaky stairs to her bedroom. The house felt even colder than before, with a chill that seemed to seep from the walls themselves. The shadows had grown long and thick, stretching like dark fingers across the floor as the sun dipped below the horizon.

Sadie flipped on the old lamp beside her bed, casting a soft yellow glow around the room. She plopped down on the edge of her bed, kicking off her shoes, and stared at the ceiling, listening to the silence. The house was filled with little noises: the groan of the pipes, the soft rattle of the wind against the window, and that ever-present creak of the floorboards beneath her feet.

Sadie let out a sigh and sat up, her eyes drifting around her room. Boxes were still scattered across the floor, some unopened, some half-unpacked. She knew she should be trying to settle in, but she felt no motivation. Her parents were downstairs, still busy with their own tasks, their voices a soft murmur in the distance.

She rubbed her arms, feeling the goosebumps rise on her skin. The room felt cold, almost too cold, like the chill was coming up from the very ground itself. She stood up and began pacing, trying to shake off the shiver that seemed to cling to her bones. As she moved, the floorboards let out a series of high-pitched squeaks under her feet, like a mouse caught in a trap.

She paused and looked down. The floor had been making strange noises ever since they had moved in, but this time it felt different. She stepped again, and the same squeak echoed through the room. She frowned, curiosity beginning to stir in her chest, and took a few more steps, her feet moving slowly over the old wood. The squeak sounded again, louder this time, coming from the centre of the room.

Sadie crouched down, running her hand over the floor, feeling the smooth surface of the planks. There was one spot that seemed to give just a little under her hand, like it wasn't quite as solid as the rest. She pressed down harder, and the wood groaned softly, as if it were tired of holding a secret for too long.

Her heart began to race. What if there was something hidden underneath? She leaned closer, pressing her ear to the floor, and gave it a small knock. The sound echoed back, hollow and deep. There was definitely something there. Sadie's fingers trembled with excitement as she traced the edges of the loose board. It seemed to be just slightly out of place, as if it could be pried up with the right amount of pressure.

She glanced around the room, her eyes landing on the metal letter opener she'd used to open some of the moving boxes. Grabbing it, she slipped the flat end under the loose board and pushed down carefully. The wood creaked and groaned, resisting at first, but then, with a soft pop, it lifted just enough for Sadie to get her fingers underneath.

Her heart pounded in her chest as she pried the board up, revealing a small, dark space underneath. She leaned in closer, squinting into the dimness. At first, she saw nothing but darkness, but then, slowly, her eyes adjusted, and she could make out the shapes of something tucked away inside.

She reached down, her hand trembling, and felt the rough edges of paper. She pulled out a small stack of yellowed envelopes, tied together with a faded red ribbon. The letters looked old, the paper brittle and stained with age, as if they had been hidden away for a very long time.

Sadie sat back on her heels, staring at the bundle in her hands. Her breath caught in her throat. Who had hidden these here? And why? Her fingers fumbled with the ribbon, pulling it loose, and the letters fell into her lap. The top one was dated December 1st, twenty-five years ago, written in a child's uneven handwriting.

She carefully unfolded it, the paper crackling softly in her hands, and began to read:

Dear Father Christmas,

I have been a very good girl this year. I promise.

For Christmas, could I please have a new doll? The one with the yellow dress like the one in the store window. I will love her so much and take care of her, I promise. Thank you, Father Christmas.

Love, Evelyn.

Sadie's eyes widened. A letter to Father Christmas? And from so long ago. She flipped to the next letter, noticing that it was dated a year later, in the same immature handwriting, though it looked a little neater:

Dear Father Christmas,

I really tried my best to be good this year.

I hope you remember me. I didn't get the doll I asked for last year, but that's okay. Maybe this year I could have a teddy bear? A soft one, with brown fur and a red ribbon around its neck. I would love him so much.

Love, Evelyn.

Sadie read the next few letters, each one dated a year apart, and each one becoming more desperate. Each letter was filled with simple wishes, things that seemed so small, yet so important to the girl who had written them.

The second-to-last letter, dated 18 years ago, looked worn and frayed, as if it had been handled more times than the others:

Dear Father Christmas,

It's me again, Evelyn. I'm not sure if you're getting my letters, but I wanted to try one more time. Things have been really hard this year. My parents... they don't really care about Christmas. They don't care about me much either. I have to do all the chores in the house — washing dishes, cleaning the floors, even cooking sometimes. They never remember my birthday, and there's never any cake or candles.

They don't even have a Christmas tree. We never put up lights or decorations. Every night, I listen to them arguing and shouting, and sometimes I have to hide in my room. My clothes are old and don't fit, and the other kids laugh at me. All I really wanted was something to make me feel less alone — a teddy bear, a new doll, anything. But it's okay. I'm used to it. Maybe... maybe you can bring me a little bit of happiness this year, please?

Love, Evelyn.

Sadie felt her chest tighten, and her eyes prickled with tears. This letter was different from the others. It was like a window into Evelyn's lonely world, filled with sadness and neglect. She could almost hear Evelyn's small, hopeful voice, even as her words spoke of disappointment and hardship. She wondered how it must have felt to write those letters year after year, only to feel like no one was listening.

Sadie's fingers trembled as she reached for the last letter, dated 17 years ago. The handwriting was more mature, but still unmistakably Evelyn's. This one seemed even sadder than the last:

Dear Father Christmas,

I guess this is it — my last letter. I'm sorry to bother you again, but I don't know who else to ask. My parents don't care about Christmas, or birthdays, or anything. They don't even see me. They just yell, and sometimes they... they hit me if I don't do things right. I don't have any toys, no dolls or bears. I don't have any friends either.

I thought if I just asked, if I kept asking, you might hear me. I thought maybe you could send me a bike or something, just so I could ride away and feel free for a while. I wanted a bike with a pretty little bell and pink streamers on the handlebars, the kind I've seen other kids have. I wanted to feel like I mattered to someone, even if it was just you. But I guess you're too busy, or maybe I'm not worth it.

I know now that I'll never get the things I asked for. I don't believe in Christmas anymore. I don't believe in magic, and I don't believe in you. This is my last letter. Goodbye,

Evelyn.

Sadie stared at the letter, feeling a heavy weight settle in her chest. She could hardly breathe, her heart aching for this little girl who had poured her heart into these letters, year after year, hoping for something better, something magical — and had only found more sadness and loneliness. She could almost feel Evelyn's hopelessness, the way her hope had slowly been crushed, letter by letter.

She folded the letters back together, tears blurring her vision. She couldn't just leave this alone. Evelyn had believed in something — in magic, in kindness — and then had that belief shattered. Sadie knew she had to do something. She had to find out what happened to Evelyn. She had to find a way to help, to restore some of that lost magic, not just for Evelyn, but for herself as well.

She hugged the letters close to her chest, feeling a wave of determination wash over her. She had to find out what happened to Evelyn. Maybe she could still help her, somehow. Maybe she could bring back the magic of Christmas for her, even if it was years too late.

Sadie stood up, pacing back and forth in her room, her mind racing with thoughts. She had to talk to someone, but who? Her parents were too busy, and they wouldn't understand. And Miss Jeffers? She'd probably just dismiss it as nonsense.

Then she thought of Emma, the girl from the bus. Maybe she would help. She seemed kind and maybe just curious enough to want to know more. Sadie grabbed her coat and slipped the letters into her pocket, ready to start her mission.

As she headed toward the door, she glanced out the window, up at the dark sky filled with stars. She knew this wasn't going to be easy. She knew finding Evelyn, wherever she was, wouldn't happen overnight. But something inside her told her she had to try.

And as she drifted off to sleep, she dreamed of snowflakes and starry skies, of letters sent and received, and a little girl's wish finally coming true.

Chapter 4

A New Mission

Sadie awoke the next morning with the first light of dawn streaming through the curtains. Her eyes blinked open, her mind still foggy from sleep, but the moment she remembered the letters, she sat up quickly, her heart heavy with thoughts of Evelyn. The little girl who had lived in this very house — who had hoped and wished for just a little bit of magic in her life, but had found none.

She looked around her bedroom, seeing the same worn walls, the same squeaky floorboards, and tried to imagine what it must have been like for Evelyn all those years ago. What kind of life had she endured here, feeling unloved, unwanted, and unseen? Sadie shivered, not just from the morning chill but from the thought of Evelyn's lonely Christmases.

Sadie swung her feet out of bed and tiptoed to the spot where she had found the letters, running her fingers over the rough edges of the floorboard. "Her parents must have hidden them," she whispered to herself. "Why else would Evelyn's letters never reach Father Christmas?"

Sadie felt a wave of anger. How could anyone be so cruel as to keep a child's letters from Father Christmas? She imagined Evelyn, year after year, carefully writing out her wishes, sealing them in envelopes, only to have them stashed away under the floorboards by people who were supposed to care for her. Sadie felt a knot tighten in her stomach. She needed to do something. She needed to find Evelyn and bring her some kind of happiness.

Downstairs, she heard the soft murmur of voices, a few laughs breaking through the stillness of the morning. Her parents were up, sharing a rare moment of peace. Sadie hesitated, then crept to the top of the stairs and peeked around the banister.

Her mother was sitting at the kitchen table, her hair still tousled from sleep, smiling at something her dad had said. Her father, his tie already loosely knotted around his neck, chuckled as he poured coffee into two mugs. They looked tired, yes, but also happy — happier than they had seemed in weeks.

Sadie felt a pang of guilt in her chest. She realised that her parents weren't ignoring her because they didn't care; they were just overwhelmed with the move, their new jobs, and the chaos of settling into a new place. They might be busy, but they still loved her deeply. She was lucky. Lucky to have parents who, despite everything, still found time to laugh together. Lucky to have people who wanted her to be happy, who tried their best for her, even when things were tough.

With a deep breath, she stepped down the stairs. Her parents looked up, smiles spreading across their faces.

"Morning, sweetheart!" her dad greeted her, his voice warm. "You're up early."

Sadie smiled back. "Morning." She took a seat at the table and looked at her mum, who slid a plate of toast in front of her. She wanted to try again, to see if her parents were up for decorating the house this morning. "I was thinking," Sadie began slowly, "Can we decorate the house this morning? It feels...empty without it."

Her mum glanced at her dad, and for a moment, there was a flicker of hesitation. "Oh, honey," her mum said gently, "We still don't have time-we've been so busy. I'm not sure when we'll have time now. But maybe you could start decorating on your own? You could pick a spot and make it special."

Sadie nodded, trying to hide her disappointment. She knew her parents were doing their best, but it still hurt a little. "Okay," she said softly, "I can do that."

"Make it as magical as you like," her dad added, giving her a wink. "We trust your taste."

She smiled, feeling a bit better. At least they cared enough to let her take charge. She finished her breakfast quickly, her thoughts already racing back to the letters and Evelyn.

When she got to school, the morning air was sharp and cold. Sadie tightened her scarf around her neck. She made her way to her classroom, her footsteps echoing through the hall. The walls seemed bare and colourless, and the grey sky outside cast a gloomy shadow over everything.

Miss Jeffers was already at her desk, her face set in its usual stern expression. She glanced up as the students shuffled in, her eyes narrowed. Sadie took her seat, feeling the usual knot of anxiety in her stomach. She glanced around the room, noticing how dreary it felt without a single Christmas decoration in sight.

She hesitated, then raised her hand. "Miss Jeffers?" she began cautiously.

"Yes, Sadie?" Miss Jeffers replied, her tone flat and uninterested.

"Would it be okay if we made some Christmas decorations for the classroom? It might make things feel... a bit more cheerful?" Sadie asked, her voice full of hope.

Miss Jeffers frowned, her lips tightening into a thin line. "Christmas decorations?" she repeated, as if the words were foreign to her. "I think that's a waste of time. We are here to learn, not to play. If you want to make decorations, do it at home. This is a classroom, not a party."

Sadie felt her heart sink. The room felt colder, even darker than before. She looked around, seeing some of the other students' faces fall. Miss Jeffers was like a wall of ice, impenetrable and unyielding. No wonder the class felt so lifeless.

She looked down at her desk, her face filled with disappointment. Miss Jeffers had just confirmed what Sadie already knew — there was no Christmas spirit here, at least not yet. She would have to find a way to change that.

At break time, Sadie found Emma by the swings, bundled up in her coat and hat. Emma waved her over with a bright smile. "Hey, Sadie! How's it going?"

Sadie took a deep breath. "There's something I need to tell you. Something... strange," she began.

Emma's eyes widened with curiosity. "Ooh, sounds exciting. What is it?"

Sadie pulled the letters from her pocket and handed them to Emma. "I found these under the floorboards in my room. They're letters to Father

Christmas... from a girl named Evelyn. They're really old, from twenty-five years ago."

Emma carefully unfolded the letters, her eyes scanning the pages. Her face grew more serious as she read, and she glanced back up at Sadie with a mix of surprise and concern. "These are so sad," she whispered. "Poor Evelyn."

"I know," Sadie said, her voice low. "I think her parents must have hidden the letters and never sent them to Father Christmas. She sounded so lonely, Emma. I want to find her. I want to show her that Christmas magic is real, even after all this time."

Emma shook her head slowly. "I don't know anyone named Evelyn. My family has lived here all my life, and I've never heard that name before."

Sadie felt a small pang of disappointment. "Oh," she murmured. "I thought maybe someone in town would remember her."

Emma looked thoughtful. "You know, this town isn't really big on Christmas," she said. "Most people don't do much. It's not like in the movies with all the lights and caroling. So, I doubt anyone else will be interested in the letters."

Sadie sighed, feeling a heavy weight settle in her chest. She had hoped Emma might have some clues, but it seemed like finding Evelyn was going to be even harder than she'd thought.

Emma brightened up suddenly and gave Sadie a playful nudge. "You know what you should do? Write to Father Christmas!" she exclaimed with a grin. "If anyone can help, it's him."

Sadie chuckled. "Write to Father Christmas?"

"Why not?" Emma said, shrugging. "I mean, it couldn't hurt. Besides, you're already on a mission to find someone who believed in him, right? Maybe he'll send some help your way."

Sadie nodded slowly. "Maybe you're right," she said thoughtfully. "I guess it's worth a shot."

Emma smiled and squeezed Sadie's hand. "Keep me updated, okay? I want to know if you find anything."

Sadie nodded, a small smile forming on her lips. "I will. Thanks, Emma."

As they walked back to class, Sadie's mind was spinning with ideas. She knew now that her mission was bigger than just finding Evelyn. If this town had lost its Christmas spirit, maybe it was up to her to bring it back. She would have to start somewhere, and maybe, just maybe, a letter to Father Christmas was exactly the place to begin.

She felt a new determination building inside her. She wasn't just going to help Evelyn. She was going to help everyone — even Miss Jeffers. She would bring back the spirit of Christmas to this sleepy, forgotten town, no matter what it took. And somehow, she knew, Father Christmas would help her find a way.

CHAPTER 5

A LETTER TO
FATHER CHRISTMAS

Sadie sat at her desk, her fingers tapping against the wooden surface, her eyes staring blankly at the paper in front of her. The room around her was silent except for the occasional creak of the old house settling in for the night. She felt a flutter of excitement and a little twinge of nerves as she picked up her pencil.

Evelyn's letters, with their faded ink and heart-wrenching words, sat beside her. She had read them over and over, each time feeling a deeper sadness for the lonely little girl who had once lived in this house. But instead of feeling discouraged, Sadie felt more determined than ever. She had to do something. She had to find Evelyn, somehow bring back the Christmas magic she had lost so long ago.

She glanced out her window, where the moon hung high in the night sky, casting a silver glow across the snow-covered garden below. The world looked still and quiet, like it was holding its breath, waiting for something wonderful to happen.

Taking a deep breath, Sadie began to write:

Dear Father Christmas,

My name is Sadie, and I recently moved to a new town with my family. At first, I was feeling a little lost and lonely because everything here is so different. But then I found some letters — letters from a girl named Evelyn, who lived in this house over twenty years ago. She wrote to you every year, asking for small things like a doll, a toy, or a bike. But she never got what she asked for, and it seems her parents didn't care about her very much.

Evelyn's letters became sadder each year, and eventually, she stopped writing altogether. I think her parents must have hidden her letters and not sent them to you, Father Christmas. I feel so sorry for Evelyn. She didn't get to feel the magic of Christmas. I want to find her and help her believe again. I think she needs to know that someone out there cares for her and that the magic she believed in can still be real.

Father Christmas, I don't know how to find Evelyn on my own. I need your help. Please, if you can, send some Christmas magic my way so I can help Evelyn and bring back the spirit of Christmas to this town. I promise I'll do my best. I just need a little bit of your magic.

With hope and kindness,
Sadie

Sadie sat back and read over her letter. It felt right. She carefully folded it into an envelope, then wrote "Father Christmas, North Pole" in her neatest handwriting across the front.

She tiptoed to the window and pushed it open, letting in a cold breeze that sent shivers down her spine. The stars glittered like diamonds in the deep blue sky, and Sadie felt a rush of anticipation. She placed the letter on the windowsill, her breath forming small clouds in the air.

She closed her eyes and whispered, "Please, Father Christmas, if you can hear me... help me find Evelyn. Help me bring back the Christmas spirit."

Sadie watched the letter for a moment, half-expecting something magical to happen right away, but everything remained still. She shut the window and crawled back into bed, pulling the blankets up to her chin. She lay there, listening to the quiet of the house, her heart fluttering with hope. As she drifted off to sleep, she wished with all her might that Father Christmas would hear her plea.

The next morning, Sadie woke up to the sound of a faint jingle. She blinked, rubbing her eyes, wondering if she was still dreaming. The room seemed brighter, almost glowing with a soft, golden light. She sat up, her eyes darting around in confusion. Then, she saw him.

Standing at the foot of her bed was the tiniest, most cheerful little figure she had ever seen. He was no more than two feet tall, with pointy ears that peeked out from under a green felt hat adorned with a red pom-pom. His cheeks were rosy, his nose slightly upturned, and his eyes sparkled like tiny stars. He wore a bright red and green outfit, and a small set of golden bells jingled around his waist with every move he made.

"Good morning, Sadie!" the little figure announced in a high, cheerful voice. "I'm Noel, one of Father Christmas's helpers. And I've come to help you with your very important mission!"

Sadie gasped, her eyes wide. "You... you're an elf!" she stammered, hardly believing her eyes.

Noel grinned, a twinkle in his eye. "That's right! And I'm here because Father Christmas got your letter. He thinks what you're doing is wonderful, and he wanted to send some help. So, here I am!" He did a little twirl, his bells ringing merrily.

Sadie's heart leapt with excitement. "You mean... Father Christmas actually read my letter?" she asked, still in disbelief.

"Of course, he did!" Noel replied, nodding eagerly. "Father Christmas reads every letter. And yours was especially important because it wasn't just about asking for presents. You wanted to help someone else, and that's the truest Christmas spirit there is!"

Sadie beamed, feeling warmth spread through her chest. "So, you're here to help me find Evelyn?" she asked.

"Absolutely!" Noel said, his eyes shining. "But there's something you should know first, Sadie. I have a special invisibility spell on me, so only you can see and hear me. This way, I can help without anyone getting suspicious. It's a neat little trick we elves have up our sleeves!"

Sadie giggled. "That's amazing! But... where do we start? I don't know where Evelyn is or even if she still lives in this town."

Noel rubbed his tiny chin, thinking. "Well, we'll need to start by gathering some clues. We'll have to look around, talk to people, and see if anyone remembers her. We'll also need to figure out why this town doesn't celebrate Christmas like other places. There's a reason why the spirit is so low here, and I think it might be connected to Evelyn somehow."

Sadie nodded, determination building in her chest. "I'm ready. Whatever we need to do, I'm in."

"That's the spirit!" Noel cheered. "First things first, though — we need to brighten up this house! You said your parents wanted you to handle the decorating, right? Well, let's get started! Nothing attracts Christmas magic like a bit of sparkle and cheer!"

Sadie jumped out of bed, feeling a burst of energy. She had a new friend, a magical helper, and a mission that filled her heart with purpose. Together with Noel, she knew she could find Evelyn and restore the joy of Christmas to everyone in town.

Sadie and Noel spent the morning rummaging through boxes in the attic, pulling out old decorations covered in dust. Sadie sneezed as she opened a box filled with tinsel and wreaths. "Wow, these look ancient!" she laughed.

Noel chuckled. "A little dust never hurt anyone! Besides, with a bit of love and a sprinkle of magic, these decorations will shine as good as new!"

They hung garlands across the windows, strung twinkling lights around the banister, and placed a small, delicate angel on the mantel. Noel used his tiny hands to fluff up an old, artificial Christmas tree they found in the corner, and with a quick snap of his fingers, the tree lit up with glowing lights and sparkling ornaments.

Sadie stared in awe. "How did you...?"

Noel winked. "A little elf magic, of course! Now, let's spread this cheer beyond these walls. We've got work to do!"

By the time Sadie's parents returned home, the house was a festive wonderland. Her mum gasped in delight, and her dad's eyes twinkled with surprise. "Wow, Sadie! This is incredible!" her mum exclaimed, pulling her into a hug. "You did all this by yourself?"

Sadie smiled, glancing at Noel, who was perched invisibly on the mantel, grinning from ear to ear. "Well, I had a little help," she replied mysteriously.

Her dad chuckled. "However you did it, it's amazing. This place feels like Christmas now."

Sadie felt a warm glow spread through her heart. For the first time since they moved, she felt truly at home. And she knew, with Noel by her side, they were just getting started on their magical mission.

Chapter 6

Uncovering the Mystery

The next morning, Sadie woke up with a renewed sense of purpose. She had barely slept a wink, her mind buzzing with ideas and plans for finding Evelyn. She looked around her room, now filled with the twinkling lights and decorations she and Noel had put up. The house felt warmer, more inviting, as if a tiny piece of Christmas magic had finally crept in.

Noel was already perched on the windowsill, his eyes twinkling with excitement. "Ready for our adventure, Sadie?" he asked, his voice full of mischief.

Sadie nodded eagerly. "Absolutely! Where do we start?"

Noel hopped down and gave a little tap dance on the floorboards. "Well, we need to start gathering some clues. Let's head into town and see what we can find out about Evelyn and her family. Maybe someone remembers something that could help us."

Sadie quickly dressed in a warm sweater, pulled on her boots, and grabbed her winter coat. She tiptoed down the stairs, careful not to wake her parents, who were enjoying a rare Saturday morning sleep-in. Noel floated beside her, invisible to everyone else, but Sadie could feel his presence like a comforting warmth.

As they stepped outside, the cold December air nipped at Sadie's cheeks. The town lay spread out before them, covered in a light dusting of snow. It looked quiet and sleepy, with only a few people bustling about, carrying their morning errands.

Sadie wandered down the main street, her eyes scanning the rows of quaint shops and cottages that lined the cobblestone path. She needed to find more clues about Evelyn, and she hoped the friendly townspeople might offer some answers.

As she turned a corner, a delicious aroma of freshly baked bread filled the air, making her stomach grumble. A small bakery with a painted wooden sign reading *Bramblewood Bakes* caught her eye. The windows were misty with warmth, and through them, Sadie could see rows of tempting pastries and a man standing behind the counter with a friendly smile. Deciding to take a chance, she pushed open the door, a small bell jingling as she entered.

"Hello there!" the man greeted warmly. "What can I do for you, young lady?"

Sadie smiled back, feeling comforted by the inviting smells and the friendly atmosphere. "Hi! I'm looking for someone... a lady named Evelyn. She would be about 29 years old now and grew up here a long time ago. Do you know her?"

The man paused, frowning slightly as he considered. "Evelyn... Evelyn..." He rubbed his chin thoughtfully. "I don't remember a girl named Evelyn around here when I was younger. She'd be my age, you say?"

Sadie nodded, a flicker of disappointment in her chest. But before she could lose hope, the man's face brightened. "But you know, my dad might know something. He's the owner of this bakery and has lived in Bramblewood his whole life, too. He remembers almost everyone. He's just resting upstairs now — doctor's orders. He's been under the weather lately, what with the stress of running this place and all, but I'll ask him later. Maybe he'll remember the family you're looking for."

"That would be great!" Sadie replied, a small flame of hope flickering back to life. She shifted her weight and then, almost without thinking, asked, "Why doesn't the town really celebrate Christmas? It seems... well... different from other towns, like there's no holiday spirit."

Jack's smile faded slightly, and he let out a small sigh. "Ah, well, it's a tough time of year for many of us here. Lots of small businesses like ours struggle to make ends meet, and spending money on decorations or events feels like a waste when you're just trying to get by. Not everyone can afford to do much, so... Christmas tends to come and go without much fuss."

Sadie nodded, understanding a little more about the challenges this town faced. "That's sad," she murmured. "Christmas should be a time for joy and celebration..."

Jack's smile returned, softer this time. "You're right, kid. It should be. And who knows, maybe you'll help bring a little cheer back to Bramblewood. Good luck finding Evelyn. And remember, you're welcome to pop in for a pastry anytime."

Sadie thanked him and left the bakery, a mix of thoughts swirling in her mind. The more she learned about this town and its people, the more determined she felt to uncover the truth about Evelyn — and maybe, just maybe, bring a little Christmas spirit back to Bramblewood.

Next, Sadie decided to ask at the local café, a small, cozy place on the corner of the main street. It had a large sign that read "Granny May's Teapot," and the windows were fogged up with warmth from inside. Sadie could see a handful of people inside, sipping coffee and chatting.

Sadie pushed open the door, and a little bell tinkled overhead. The smell of freshly baked cinnamon rolls and hot cocoa filled the air. An elderly woman behind the counter, with a kind face and a floral apron, looked up and smiled warmly.

"Hello there, dear!" the woman called out. "I don't think I've seen you around before."

Sadie stepped up to the counter, her heart beating a little faster. "Hi, I'm Sadie. My family just moved into the old house on Elm Street. I was wondering if you knew anything about the family who lived there before us, a girl named Evelyn?"

The woman's face softened with a distant look, as if she were searching her memories. "Evelyn, you say? Oh, I think I do remember a little girl by that name. But it was so long ago... she was very quiet, kept to herself mostly. Lived in that house with her father, the mayor at the time."

Sadie's eyes widened. "The mayor? What happened to him?"

The woman sighed, shaking her head slowly. "Oh, it's a sad story, that one. The mayor was disgraced about ten years ago. There were whispers of some scandal, but no one knew the full truth. He just up and left town one night, disappeared without a trace. Took Evelyn with him, I reckon. I don't think I ever saw that poor girl again."

Sadie's heart sank. The story seemed to get more complicated with each turn. "Did anyone else know her? Was she friends with anyone?"

The woman shook her head again. "No, I don't think so, dear. She was a shy thing, kept to herself. I remember seeing her around sometimes, but she never spoke much. It was as if she was... almost invisible."

Sadie thanked the woman and turned to Noel, who had been listening quietly from a corner. "That wasn't much help," she whispered, feeling a little defeated.

Noel gave her a reassuring smile. "Don't worry, Sadie. We're just getting started. Let's try the library next. It's the best place to find out more about this town's history."

Sadie nodded, feeling a surge of determination. "You're right. Let's go!"

The library was a grand old building, its red bricks covered in ivy, with tall windows that seemed to watch over the town like wise old eyes. Inside, it was quiet and smelled of aged paper and polished wood. Rows upon rows of books lined the shelves, towering over them like ancient guardians of secrets.

Sadie and Noel headed to the front desk, where a librarian with round glasses and a knitted cardigan was busy stacking books. Sadie cleared her throat. "Excuse me, could you help me find some information about the town's past? Maybe about the old mayor and his family?"

The librarian peered over her glasses, eyeing Sadie curiously. "Ah, the old mayor... a troubled man, that one. We have some old newspapers and yearbooks in the archives that might help. You're welcome to have a look."

She led them to a small room at the back of the library, filled with dusty volumes and yellowed newspapers. Sadie felt a little thrill as she entered, like she was stepping back in time.

Noel fluttered up to a high shelf, pulling down a stack of newspapers with surprising strength for his tiny size. "Let's start here!" he chirped, his bells jingling softly.

Sadie and Noel continued searching through the newspapers and old documents, their fingers covered in dust and their eyes straining in the dim light. The hours seemed to drag by, with only the quiet rustle of pages filling the air. Sadie was beginning to feel a bit discouraged. Maybe there was nothing here that could help them after all.

Just as she was about to give up, Sadie's hand brushed against an old yearbook buried beneath a stack of crumbling papers. Its once-bright cover had faded to a dull, worn blue, and the pages crackled softly as she opened it. She flipped through it slowly, her heart beating a little faster with every page she turned.

And then she saw it—a small black-and-white photograph of a young girl with wide, haunting eyes and light, wavy hair that framed her delicate face. The girl seemed familiar, almost like a whisper of a memory Sadie couldn't quite grasp. She leaned in closer, studying the photo carefully.

Beneath the photograph was a name: *Evelyn Roberts.*

Sadie looked confused. Noel flitted over to her shoulder, peering at the photo.

Sadie shook her head. "I don't know... but there's something about her face. I feel like I've seen it before, somewhere else. But where?"

She thought back to all the places she'd been in town, all the people she had met since moving here, but she couldn't quite place the girl in the photo. It was like trying to remember a dream that kept slipping away.

Noel tapped his chin thoughtfully. "This could be a clue, Sadie. Maybe Evelyn goes by a different name now. Either way, we're getting closer. We just have to keep looking."

Sadie nodded, a mix of determination and curiosity bubbling inside her. "You're right, Noel. There's more to this story. We need to find out who Evelyn Roberts is- I think she is still here. Maybe it will help us understand why the town lost its Christmas spirit."

Noel's smile returned, full of encouragement. "I have a feeling we're on the right path. Let's keep searching, and soon we'll uncover all the secrets hidden in this town."

Sadie carefully closed the yearbook and tucked it under her arm. She felt a renewed sense of purpose, like a tiny spark of magic flickering to life inside her. AT least they now knew who they were looking for. She knew that they were getting closer to the truth, and she was ready for whatever came next.

With Noel by her side, she was determined to unravel the mystery of Evelyn—and perhaps find a way to restore the Christmas spirit that had been lost for so long.

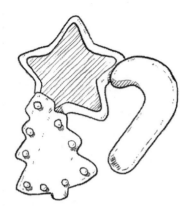

CHAPTER 7

BRINGING CHRISTMAS CHEER

Sadie walked to school the next morning with a bounce in her step, clutching a bag full of colourful paper, scissors, and homemade cookies. She was more determined than ever to spread some Christmas cheer, even if it meant going against the gloomy atmosphere of Miss Jeffers' classroom. The cold December air made her face sting, but it only made her feel more alive, more ready for what she was about to do.

When Sadie entered the classroom, it felt as though a cloud had settled over the room. The grey walls seemed to close in, and the air was thick with silence. Miss Jeffers stood at her desk, her expression as chilly as a winter morning. Sadie could see a small frown forming on her lips as she noticed Sadie's arms full of supplies.

"Good morning, everyone!" Sadie chirped, trying to sound as cheerful as she could. She set her things down on her desk and immediately got to work, cutting and folding the paper into delicate snowflakes. Each snip of the scissors sent tiny flakes of paper fluttering to the floor like the first snowfall of winter. She then carefully arranged the cookies on a plate, their warm, sugary smell spreading throughout the room like a comforting hug.

Some of her classmates glanced over, curious. A boy named Max leaned over his desk. "What are you doing, Sadie?" he whispered, eyes wide with interest.

"Making some decorations for the room!" Sadie replied with a grin. "I thought it could use a bit of Christmas spirit, don't you?"

Max nodded eagerly. "Can I make one too?"

Sadie beamed. "Of course! Here, take some paper."

Slowly, more kids began to drift over, curiosity sparkling in their eyes like twinkling lights on a Christmas tree. They started folding and cutting, and soon, colourful paper snowflakes and chains were being made all around the classroom. The room seemed to brighten with each new decoration, the once-dull atmosphere lifting little by little. Even the shyest kids, like Lily and Ben, were giggling and helping out.

The cookies were passed around, and the children's laughter filled the room, warm and sweet, like the scent of cinnamon wafting through a cosy kitchen.

But just as Sadie was starting to feel like her plan was working, a sharp voice cut through the chatter like a cold wind. "What is going on here?" Miss Jeffers' voice was harsh and clipped, her eyes narrowing as she approached the group.

The classroom fell silent. The laughter died, and the colourful decorations seemed to wilt under Miss Jeffers' icy glare.

Sadie stood up, her heart pounding in her chest. "We were just... just trying to bring a little Christmas cheer, Miss Jeffers," she explained, her voice quivering a bit.

Miss Jeffers' face grew even more pinched. "Christmas cheer?" she scoffed, her voice hard as frost. "Haven't I already made it clear, Sadie-this is a classroom, not a holiday fair. We are here to learn, not waste time on... on frivolities." She snatched a paper snowflake from a child's hand and crumpled it into a tight ball.

The room seemed to grow darker, the air colder, as Miss Jeffers moved to the front of the class. She pointed at the decorations with a demanding finger. "Everyone, back to your seats. And you," she added, looking straight at Sadie, "stop this nonsense at once. I don't want to hear another word about Christmas, do you understand?"

Sadie swallowed hard and nodded, her cheeks flushing with embarrassment. She could feel all eyes on her, and her heart sank like a stone in her chest. She had tried so hard to make things a little brighter, but it seemed like Miss Jeffers' shadow was too heavy, too strong.

As the children returned to their seats, Sadie noticed something—something subtle, but there all the same. Whenever Christmas was mentioned, whenever someone spoke of decorations or gifts or holiday cheer, Miss Jeffers' face grew even colder, her mouth tightening into a thin line. It was as if just the word "Christmas" stung like an icy wind.

There was something more to Miss Jeffers' reaction, Sadie realised. It was almost as if Christmas caused her pain. Sadie's heart softened just a little. Maybe, just maybe, there was a reason for her harshness.

After class, Sadie caught up with Emma in the playground. "She really hates Christmas," Sadie whispered, glancing back at the classroom window where Miss Jeffers stood, watching them with her arms crossed.

Emma nodded. "Yeah, she's always like that. Every year, she gets grumpier around Christmas time. It's like she doesn't want anyone to have fun."

Sadie noticed something strange in Miss Jeffers' eyes. As the teacher stared at her, there was a flicker of something beneath the sternness—anxiety, perhaps, or even fear. Her eyes seemed oddly familiar, like Sadie had seen them somewhere before. And there it was—a flash of pain that Sadie recognised, the kind she had seen in the photograph of the girl in the yearbook, the same deep sadness that seemed to linger like a shadow.

Miss Jeffers quickly turned away, her face becoming a mask of cold indifference once more.

Sadie felt a shiver run down her spine. She was sure of it now—she had seen that look before, and it was not just sadness; it was the same deep, aching loneliness that had filled Evelyn's letters.

And now she had more questions than ever.

CHAPTER 8

A PLAN TO BRING BACK CHRISTMAS

Sadie burst through the front door, her heart pounding with excitement. The winter air made her eyes water, but she hardly noticed. She ran up the stairs, taking them two at a time, and flung open the door to her room. Noel was perched on the windowsill, his small, pointy hat tilted back as he gazed out at the snowy landscape. He turned around as soon as she entered, his eyes twinkling with curiosity.

"Noel! I think I know who Miss Jeffers really is!" Sadie gasped, barely able to catch her breath. "I think she's Evelyn! The girl from the letters!"

Noel's face lit up with excitement. "You're sure?" he asked, hopping down from the windowsill and landing lightly on the floor. His tiny bells jingled as he moved closer.

"Yes! When I was at school today, I noticed something in her eyes. It was the same look I saw in that old yearbook picture. I think she's the girl who wrote those letters to Father Christmas," Sadie explained, her voice filled with a mix of wonder and determination. "It's like she's been carrying this sadness around for years."

Noel nodded, his face serious now. "If Miss Jeffers really is Evelyn, then it makes sense why she doesn't like Christmas. She lost her faith in it a long time ago. But maybe... maybe we can help her find it again."

Sadie grinned. "That's what I was thinking! But we can't just walk up to her and say, 'Hey, we know you're Evelyn, and we're going to make you believe in Christmas again.' We have to warm up her heart first."

Noel giggled. "That might be a bit much, yeah. So, what's the plan?"

Sadie's mind was racing with ideas. "I think we need to start with the town. Miss Jeffers isn't the only one who's lost the Christmas spirit. The whole place seems... well, like it's forgotten how to celebrate. We need to bring everyone together, make them feel the magic of Christmas again."

Noel's eyes sparkled. "A town-wide plan, eh? I like it! So, what do you have in mind?"

Sadie quickly grabbed a notebook and pen from her desk and started jotting down ideas. "We could organise a Christmas Town Fair! We'll invite everyone to come together—there'll be carol singers, a tree lighting ceremony, hot chocolate, gingerbread, and festive games. Everyone could volunteer to run a stall, like a bake sale or a craft booth. We could even have a sleigh ride!"

Noel clapped his hands with glee. "That sounds perfect! And it's just the thing to spread some Christmas cheer."

Sadie's eyes twinkled as she continued, "And we'll make sure Miss Jeffers is at the centre of it. We could send her a special, anonymous invitation, asking her to turn on the Christmas lights as an 'upstanding member of the town.' It might just remind her of what it feels like to be part of something joyful and warm."

Noel nodded, his face glowing with excitement. "Yes! If she feels important and included, it might start to soften that icy shell of hers. Let's get to work!"

The two of them spent the next hour crafting a bright, festive poster. Sadie's hands moved quickly, drawing cheerful snowmen, candy canes, and a big, bold title: **"Christmas Fair: Let's Bring the Spirit Back!"** Underneath, they added details about the event: "Carol singers, tree lighting, games, treats, and more! Sign up to run a stall and help spread the Christmas cheer!" There was a large space at the bottom for people to volunteer.

Sadie grinned at their work. "Now we just need to get these all over town!"

Noel snapped his fingers. "And I'll take care of Miss Jeffers' invitation. She won't know it's from you, but it'll be special."

They spent the rest of the afternoon making copies of the poster. Sadie could hardly contain her excitement as she and Noel snuck out and began putting them up all around town. They tacked them to notice boards, shop windows, and even on the lampposts that lined the cobblestone streets. Noel, with his invisibility, worked quickly and efficiently, adding an extra touch of magic to the whole process.

By the time they were finished, the posters were everywhere. Sadie watched as people stopped to read them, some of them raising their eyebrows in surprise, others smiling with delight. It seemed like a long time since this town had seen such excitement.

At school the next day, Sadie's eyes were fixed on Miss Jeffers as she walked into the classroom. The teacher had a letter in her hand—the invitation that Sadie and Noel had crafted. Miss Jeffers looked down at the piece of paper, her lips pressed tightly together. For a moment, Sadie thought she might tear it up, but then she noticed something—a tiny, almost imperceptible softening in Miss Jeffers' harsh expression.

Miss Jeffers cleared her throat and looked up, her gaze sweeping across the room until it landed on Sadie. Her eyes still held that familiar sadness, but there was a flicker of something else—a pretty light that had not been there before.

"I have received a request," Miss Jeffers began slowly, "for me to participate in a Christmas event as a... as a representative of the town." Her voice trembled just slightly. "I am... honoured by the gesture."

Sadie could barely contain her excitement. She exchanged a quick, thrilled glance with Noel, who winked back from his spot near the window.

Miss Jeffers took a deep breath, as if gathering her courage. "And so, I suppose, since it seems this event is meant to bring cheer... we might as well contribute." Her lips tightened, but Sadie saw that flicker again. "Today, you may all work on some posters for the Christmas Fair."

A gasp of surprise and delight rippled through the classroom. Sadie's heart leapt with joy. It wasn't much, but it was a start. And in Miss Jeffers' hesitant acceptance, Sadie could feel a crack forming in that wall around her heart—a wall that had been built up for many years.

As the class dove into making their posters, Sadie whispered to Noel, "It's working, Noel! I think it's really working."

Noel grinned. "Oh, it's just the beginning, Sadie. Just the beginning."

CHAPTER 9

THE BIG REVEAL

After break, Sadie's heart swelled with excitement as she hurried down the hallway toward her classroom. She could still see that flicker of light in Miss Jeffers' eyes—a flicker she knew was just the beginning. As she stepped inside, the room was filled with unusual sounds of laughter and chatter, as today, there was an extra layer of warmth in the air. Christmas spirit, Sadie thought with a smile.

Miss Jeffers stood at the front of the classroom, shuffling through some papers, clearly distracted.

She glanced up at the clock, a frown forming across her face. "Class, I have a meeting with the principal. I expect you all to continue working quietly on your posters," she said, her voice tinged with a hint of reluctance, as if she wasn't quite ready to leave the room.

Sadie held her breath until Miss Jeffers stepped out, the door clicking shut behind her. The moment she was gone, Sadie sprang up from her chair.

"Everyone, listen up!" she called, waving her arms to get her classmates' attention. The room fell quiet, all eyes on Sadie. She took a deep breath, her heart racing. "I've got something important to tell you."

The class leaned in, intrigued. Sadie glanced toward the door to make sure Miss Jeffers wasn't coming back too soon.

"It's about Miss Jeffers," Sadie began, lowering her voice to a conspiratorial whisper. "I know why she's been so grumpy and why she doesn't like Christmas. I think her name is... Evelyn. A girl from some letters I found in my house."

A few kids gasped, while others furrowed their brows in confusion. Emma raised her hand. "Wait, Miss Jeffers is Evelyn?"

Sadie quickly explained about the letters she had discovered—the letters from a little girl named Evelyn who had lost her faith in Christmas because she never got the gifts she asked for. She told them how each letter grew more desperate, how Evelyn seemed to feel more and more alone. And then, she dropped the revelation. "And I'm almost certain that Evelyn is our Miss Jeffers."

The room went silent, each child processing this unexpected news. Then, Jamie, a boy with a head full of wild curls, spoke up. "So... Miss Jeffers never got what she wanted for Christmas? That's why she's so grumpy?"

Sadie nodded. "I think so. And I think we can help. Maybe if we showed her that Christmas can still be magical, that it can still be full of love and kindness... maybe she'll start to believe again."

A girl named Lily, who always had the brightest smile, chimed in, "How do we do that?"

Sadie's eyes sparkled with excitement. "We write a list of what she asked for all those years ago... and we try to give it to her now. Like, recreate the presents she never got!"

The class murmured with excitement. "But how do we know what she wanted?" a boy in the back asked.

Sadie pulled out a small, crumpled piece of paper—the list she'd made of all the gifts from Evelyn's letters. "I wrote them all down. There's a doll, a teddy bear, and even a pink bike with tassels."

The room buzzed with energy as the children crowded around to see the list. Emma's eyes widened. "That's a lot of stuff... but I think we can do it! Maybe we can bring some money from our savings, or see if we have any of these things at home?"

Jamie grinned. "Yeah! I have an old teddy bear that's still in good shape. I could bring that!"

Another classmate, Bella, raised her hand. "I have a cousin who just outgrew her pink bike. Maybe I could ask my parents if we could give it to Miss Jeffers?"

Sadie beamed. "See? We can do this! We just have to work together."

The kids nodded eagerly, their faces lighting up with a sense of purpose. For the rest of the day, they whispered plans to one another, sharing ideas on how they could collect the gifts and bring a little bit of magic back into their teacher's life.

When the school day ended, Sadie hurried home, feeling a sense of joy she hadn't felt in weeks. She couldn't wait to tell Noel about everything that had happened.

As soon as she got home, she found Noel perched on her desk, looking at the poster for the Christmas Fair. "Noel! It's working!" she shouted as she ran into the room.

Noel's eyes shone with curiosity. "Tell me everything!"

Sadie told him about the class's reaction, how they were all pitching in to recreate the presents from Evelyn's letters. Noel clapped his hands with delight. "That's fantastic, Sadie! You're bringing the magic back, not just to Miss Jeffers, but to the whole class!"

"We even saw some changes in town today," Sadie added, her voice bubbling with excitement. "People are getting into the Christmas spirit! The tea shop has put up twinkling lights, and there are garlands on the bakery's windows. And the sign-up sheet for the fair is so full, it's spilled over to the back!"

Noel grinned widely. "That's the power of Christmas magic! It's contagious!"

Sadie nodded. "I think the town is finally waking up. But there's still a lot we don't know... like what happened with Evelyn's father. The Mayor left town in disgrace about ten years ago. I wonder what he did."

Noel's expression grew thoughtful. "That's a mystery we'll have to solve... but for now, we've already taken a big step forward."

Sadie felt a warm glow in her chest as she looked around her room, imagining all the faces in town lighting up with joy. She realized that by trying to bring Christmas back to one person, they were starting to bring it back to everyone.

"And maybe," she said softly, "we're starting to bring it back for ourselves, too."

Noel nodded, his eyes softening. "You're doing something special, Sadie. And I have a feeling it's only the beginning."

With that, the two of them continued to brainstorm, planning how to gather the gifts and make the Christmas Fair the best the town had ever seen. As Sadie drifted off to sleep that night, her heart felt lighter than it had in weeks, filled with hope, excitement, and the magic of Christmas.

CHAPTER 10

THE CHRISTMAS SURPRISE

Sadie could hardly believe her eyes as she walked through town on the last day of school before the holiday break. Just a few weeks ago, this place had seemed so bleak and dreary, like a snow globe without any snow. Now, it felt as if she had stepped into a magical storybook. Twinkling fairy lights crisscrossed above the streets, their soft glow casting patterns that danced on the cobblestones. The bakery's windows were frosted with intricate snowflake designs, and wreaths adorned every door, each one more beautifully decorated than the last.

The air was filled with the sound of Christmas carols, and the scent of cinnamon and pine hung in the crisp winter breeze. Shopkeepers smiled and waved as Sadie passed, their cheeks rosy from the cold and from the warmth in their hearts. Even the tea shop, which had once seemed so drab, was now bursting with holly and ivy, its windows fogged with the cosy heat from inside. Snow had blanketed the town in a soft, shimmering layer, turning the place into a true Winter Wonderland.

Sadie felt a thrill of joy rush through her. This was the kind of Christmas she had dreamed of—the kind she had thought was impossible when she first arrived in this sleepy, sad town. And the best part? It wasn't just about the decorations or the festivities. The whole town had come together, working side by side, their hearts opening like flowers in the warmth of the sun. It was as if the very air was charged with hope.

Sadie couldn't resist popping back into *Bramblewood Bakes* on her way to school. The bakery windows were frosted with the early morning chill, but inside, the warmth and the sweet scent of pastries enveloped her like a comforting blanket.

Jack, the friendly man behind the counter, looked up as she entered, his face breaking into a broad smile. "Well, look who's here! Have you come for that pastry I promised?" he teased.

Sadie laughed. "I guess I have," she replied, stepping up to the counter. "But I also wanted to see how things are going... You know, with Christmas coming up and everything."

Jack chuckled as he handed her a warm croissant, wrapped in a little napkin. "Things are... different, that's for sure. It's like you've put a magic spell on everyone since you came to town. Even my dad's feeling better. He hasn't felt this way in years — not since the business started struggling about ten years ago."

Sadie's heart warmed at his words, and she took a bite of the croissant, the buttery layers melting in her mouth. "I'm glad to hear that," she said. "Christmas should be a time for everyone to feel a little happier. I just hope it stays that way."

Jack nodded in agreement. "You're right. And it seems like this little Christmas fair has woken something up in the town. People are talking about it, and there's a real buzz around here. It's been a long time since I've seen anything like it. The bakery is also doing so well- we've been very busy!"

Sadie smiled, pleased that her efforts were making a difference. But she realised she'd better hurry or risk being late. "I should go, or Miss Jeffers won't be happy with me."

Jack's expression shifted slightly. "Oh, how is she as a teacher? I've heard she's quite strict."

Sadie hesitated for a moment. "She is... but I think she's starting to soften a little with all the Christmas magic around. Do... do people not like her much?"

Jack shrugged, his eyes clouding with a hint of sadness. "Well, not everyone knows her like I did. I liked her... in fact, I loved her once upon a time. We were supposed to be married a couple of years ago."

Sadie's eyes widened in surprise. "You were?"

Jack nodded. "Yes, but she called off the wedding out of the blue. I remember I mentioned once that we'd have to have a small wedding because my family didn't have much money... and a few days later, she ended things. Broke my heart, to be honest. I never understood why she did it."

Sadie listened, feeling a pang of sadness for Jack. "I'm sorry, Jack. That must have been so hard."

Jack smiled, though his eyes were still wistful. "It was... but life goes on. I just always wondered why. Eve — Miss Jeffers — she was never one for extravagance, so I never thought it was about the money."

Sadie nodded, feeling a knot of confusion forming in her mind. "Well, I'd better get to school," she said softly, "but thank you for the pastry... and for sharing that with me."

As Sadie left the bakery, Jack waved her off with a gentle smile. "Anytime, Sadie. And good luck with your Christmas magic." As she walked away, Jack suddenly called out, "Oh, Sadie, did you find that Evelyn girl you were looking for?"

Sadie hesitated for a moment, giving an awkward smile before replying, "I think I have a strong lead; I'm getting close now." She waved and quickly ran off to school, her mind swirling with thoughts about everything she had just discovered.

As Sadie made her way to school, she couldn't shake the feeling of sadness that had settled over her. She felt sorry for Jack, who had clearly loved Miss Jeffers deeply, not even knowing who she really was. She wondered what could have driven Evelyn to call off the wedding. It didn't seem to fit with what she had learned about Miss Jeffers so far. She wasn't the type to care about money or status... so why had she ended things with Jack?

A new layer of mystery surrounded Evelyn and her troubled life, and Sadie knew she had to dig deeper to understand. She hoped that in uncovering the truth, she could help bring some light back into Miss Jeffers' life... and perhaps restore the joy that had been lost for so long.

As she reached the school, she noticed that even Miss Jeffers seemed different. Over the past few weeks, she had slowly softened, her stern expression gradually giving way to small smiles, especially when the children spoke of the fair. Miss Jeffers had even taken on some of the planning, suggesting a bake sale and a Christmas tree decorating contest. Sadie had seen her laugh more in the last few days than she ever imagined she could.

Today, though, felt different. There was a sense of anticipation in the air, and Sadie could feel it humming in her veins. The students were buzzing with excitement, whispering and giggling in their seats as they glanced up at Miss Jeffers, who stood at her desk with her usual stack of papers.

But there was a change in Miss Jeffers. Her intense look seemed softer, almost as if she were allowing herself to hope for something she hadn't dared to hope for in a long time. As the bell rang to signal the start of the day, Sadie caught a glimpse of something—was it a sparkle?—in Miss Jeffers' eye.

Once the lessons were over and the final bell rang, Sadie stood up and cleared her throat. "Miss Jeffers," she began nervously, "we have something for you. A Christmas surprise."

Miss Jeffers looked up, clearly puzzled. "For me?" she asked, her voice uncertain.

Sadie nodded and glanced at her classmates. Together, they moved forward, each child holding a wrapped present. Miss Jeffers looked bewildered, her gaze darting between the children and the gifts. "What is this?" she whispered, her hands slightly trembling.

Sadie smiled and placed the first gift—a small, neatly wrapped package—in Miss Jeffers' hands. "Open it," she urged gently.

Miss Jeffers hesitated for a moment, then carefully peeled back the wrapping paper. Inside was a small, old-fashioned porcelain doll, dressed in a yellow dress with a lace bonnet—exactly like the one Evelyn had described in her first letter to Father Christmas.

Miss Jeffers' eyes widened in shock. She blinked rapidly, as if she couldn't quite believe what she was seeing. "But... how...?" she stammered, her voice barely above a whisper.

Before she could say more, another child handed her the second gift. This one was a little teddy bear, its fur soft and comforting, with a ribbon tied around its neck. Her breath caught as she recognised it as the teddy bear from her letter when she was six.

Her hands began to shake as she reached for the next gift, a small wooden box. She opened it, and inside was a pink bicycle bell with a tiny set of streamers—just like the ones she had begged Father Christmas for all those years ago.

Tears welled up in Miss Jeffers' eyes, threatening to spill over as she looked up at the smiling faces of her students. "How did you... how did you know?" she asked, her voice thick with emotion.

Sadie took a step forward, holding out a bundle of papers—old, worn letters, some with crinkled edges and faded ink. "I found these in my house," she explained softly. "They were letters you wrote to Father Christmas a long time ago, but they never got sent. We wanted to make sure you got what you wished for."

Miss Jeffers' trembling hand reached out, taking the letters as if they were made of the most delicate glass. Her eyes scanned the familiar handwriting, the letters she had poured her heart into so many years ago. And then, with a gasp, she noticed the yearbook that Sadie held in her other hand—the one that showed a photograph of a young girl named Evelyn Roberts.

For a moment, Miss Jeffers seemed frozen, caught between the past and the present. She stared at the letters, then at the yearbook, and finally at the children around her. Her eyes filled with tears, and she clutched the gifts close to her chest. "I never... I never thought anyone would care," she whispered, her voice breaking.

Sadie stepped closer, her own heart swelling with emotion. "We care, Miss Jeffers. And we wanted to show you that Christmas can still be magical, no matter what happened in the past."

Miss Jeffers looked around the room, at the beaming faces of her students, and something in her expression changed. The cold, guarded look she had worn for so long melted away like ice in the warmth of the sun. Her lips quivered, then turned up into a smile—a real, genuine smile that seemed to light up the entire room.

"Thank you," she whispered, her voice filled with gratitude. "Thank you so much. You've given me more than just these gifts. You've given me... hope."

The class cheered, their joy filling the room. Sadie felt a wave of warmth flood her chest. She knew now that they had not only found Evelyn, but they had also brought her back from the cold, lonely place where she had been stuck for so long. They had reminded her of the magic of Christmas—the magic that lived not in presents or decorations, but in the hearts of people who cared.

And as Miss Jeffers wiped away a tear, Sadie knew, deep down, that this was the best Christmas surprise of all.

CHAPTER 11

EVELYN'S STORY

After class, the whole school set off to Mainstreet where the Christmas Fair was in full swing, and the town was buzzing with an energy it hadn't felt in years. Stalls decorated with twinkling lights and holly were bursting with homemade crafts, hot cider, and gingerbread cookies. A choir of children sang carols, their young voices rising and falling in harmony. The large Christmas tree in the centre of the square stood proudly, its branches heavy with ornaments and garlands, waiting for the grand lighting ceremony.

Sadie watched as families gathered, laughing and enjoying the festive evening. She could hardly believe how much had changed since she arrived. Only weeks ago, this town had felt like a forgotten place, drained of life and colour. But now, it was transformed into a winter wonderland, alive with joy and the spirit of Christmas. Sadie felt her heart swell with pride, knowing she had played a part in this transformation.

But tonight wasn't just about celebrating; it was also about healing. Sadie's eyes flicked to Miss Jeffers, standing off to the side of the stage. She looked nervous, her usually stern face looked beautiful as it softened by uncertainty. Sadie could see the way her hands trembled as she clutched at her coat. She knew this was a big moment for Miss Jeffers — or rather, Evelyn.

Evelyn glanced out over the crowd, a mixture of anxiety and determination in her eyes. Her gaze met Sadie's for a brief moment, and Sadie gave her a reassuring smile. She hoped Evelyn felt the support surrounding her, the goodwill that had been built over the past weeks.

Taking a deep breath, Evelyn stepped up to the microphone, and the crowd slowly quieted. The town, eager to see the lights turned on, sensed there was something more Evelyn needed to say. Her voice wavered slightly at first, but then she began to speak with a quiet strength.

"Good evening, everyone, I feel truly honoured and touched to have been asked to turn on the Christmas lights here tonight." Evelyn began, her voice carrying over the stillness of the crowd. "But I feel I have to be honest with you all. I'm... I'm not who you all think I am." An awkward silence settled over the gathering, punctuated by a few surprised gasps. Evelyn took a deep breath, steadying herself. "For a long time, I've been hiding who I truly am, hiding from my past and from all of you. My real name is Evelyn Roberts."

A murmur rippled through the crowd. People whispered to one another, eyebrows raised in surprise. Sadie could hear a few gasps. She herself felt a flutter in her stomach; she knew this was difficult for Evelyn, but she also knew it was necessary.

Evelyn's eyes swept over the crowd. "Many of you probably don't remember me. I wouldn't blame you if you didn't. You see, I grew up here... but I was kept hidden away. My father was the mayor of this town many years ago."

Sadie watched as a few older townspeople nodded, some recognising the name and the history attached to it. Evelyn's voice grew stronger, and her hands stopped trembling. "My father was not a kind man. He banned Christmas in this town, saying it was too costly when people were struggling. But the truth was... you were struggling because he was stealing from you all. He took the town's money and hid it away for himself."

Her voice broke slightly, but she continued. "He was a harsh man at home, too. I grew up in that big old house at the end of Elm Street... the one where Sadie and her family live now. But inside, it was nothing like a home should be. My parents... they never showed me love. Not once. They ignored me, forgot my birthday year after year, and scoffed at the idea of Christmas."

Tears welled up in Evelyn's eyes, and she paused, swallowing hard before continuing. "I had to do all the housework. I wore the same ragged clothes until they were falling apart. I begged for a few toys, just something to hold on to... but there was never

98

anything. My father's cruel words and my mother's cold silence were all I knew."

Sadie could see the pain in Evelyn's eyes, the old wounds reopening as she spoke. Her voice was softer now, barely above a whisper. "I would write letters to Father Christmas every year, dreaming of a doll, a teddy, a pink bike with tassels... silly little things. I thought maybe... maybe if I just wished hard enough, something would change. But those letters never went anywhere. They were hidden away, never to be sent. My father would laugh at my hopefulness, calling it foolishness. My mother... she never said a word."

Evelyn's shoulders trembled, and she took another deep breath. The crowd stood silently, hanging on her every word. Tears glistened on more than one cheek. Even the smallest children seemed to understand the sadness in Evelyn's story.

"When I was fifteen, I couldn't stand it any longer. I felt trapped in that house, trapped by their indifference and cruelty. I ran away. I found a job in a new town, a place to live, and eventually, a new school. I trained to be a teacher, thinking I could leave all of this behind me, but... you can't escape your past so easily."

She smiled sadly, her eyes wet with tears. "I returned here five years ago, hoping maybe to make peace, to find something familiar. But when I arrived, my old house was boarded up, and my parents... they were gone. Fled with the town's money, leaving behind nothing but shame. I didn't want anyone to know who I was. So, I became Miss Eve Jeffers."

Her voice wavered again, and she wiped a tear from her cheek. Evelyn paused, the microphone trembling slightly in her hand as she gazed out over the crowd. Her eyes were filled with a mixture of pain and resolve, as if she was battling to keep her emotions under control. Sadie could see the weight of her past pressing down on her, the secrets she had kept hidden for so long now pouring out for all to hear.

"And to make my life even more devastating," Evelyn continued, her voice wavering, "A few years ago, I had finally found the love of my life, Jack. For once, I felt like I had something good — something real. He was the first person I met when I returned 5 years ago and he made me believe that I could be happy, that I could have a future here, in this very town. But he never knew who I really was!"

There was a murmur of surprise among the townspeople. Sadie glanced over at Jack, standing near the back of the crowd, his face pale and his eyes wide with shock.

Evelyn took a deep breath and continued, "But then... Jack told me one day that he didn't have much money. He said his family had struggled ever since his father's business began to decline. And I knew, deep in my heart, that it was because of what my father had done to this town all those years ago." She swallowed hard, blinking back tears. "I felt such shame, such guilt. My father's greed had caused so much suffering to you all, including Jack's father, who had even become ill from the stress of it all. I realised that if Jack found out who I really was, if he discovered that it was my father who had brought such hardship to his family, he would never want to marry me. He would hate me... just like I had hated my father."

The crowd was silent, listening intently as Evelyn bared her soul. "I couldn't bear the thought of losing Jack's love," she said, her voice cracking. "So, instead of risking being hurt again, I chose to end it myself. I pushed him away before he could push me away. I lost the only person who ever truly loved me."

Evelyn's words hung in the air like a winter fog, heavy and cold. Tears were streaming down her cheeks now, unchecked. Jack stood motionless, his face a mixture of heartbreak and understanding, as he listened to this shocking truth for the very first time.

"I thought I was protecting myself from more pain, but all I did was bring more sorrow into my life," Evelyn continued, her voice barely a whisper now. "I lived with that regret every day, shutting myself off from the world, from happiness... from Christmas, even. I've been so afraid to feel again, afraid that everything good would just slip away, like it always had."

Sadie's heart ached for Evelyn. She could see the raw pain in her teacher's eyes, the regret that had haunted her for so long. It was clear now why Evelyn had hidden herself away, why she had become so closed-off and strict. She had been protecting her heart from breaking again, like it had done, so many times before.

Evelyn paused, her gaze drifting upward to the dark winter sky. "But then... something changed. A little girl found those letters I had written all those years ago... letters that were meant for Father Christmas, letters that carried all my hope and dreams. And that same little girl decided she was going to bring Christmas back to this town... and back to me."

Evelyn looked down at Sadie, her eyes filled with gratitude. "She reminded me of what I'd lost, what I'd hidden away. The spirit of Christmas isn't about what you get or don't get. It's about love, kindness, and community. It's about reaching out and believing in one another."

Tears continued to stream down Evelyn's face, but they were tears of relief, of a weight being lifted from her shoulders. She took a step forward, extending her arms to Sadie. "I... I was so lost, but you found me. And you didn't give up on me."

Sadie, with tears in her own eyes, rushed forward and embraced Evelyn tightly. The crowd began to applaud, softly at first, then louder, until it swelled into a wave of support and love that filled the town square.

Sadie's parents stepped onto the stage, and her mother gently placed a hand on Evelyn's shoulder.

"Miss Jeffers — Evelyn — you don't have to be alone anymore. You're welcome at our home for Christmas, and anytime you want. Our door will always be open to you."

A chorus of voices rose from the crowd. "You're welcome at our house, too!" "Come to ours for Christmas dinner!" "You've got a place with us!"

Evelyn's face was a mix of disbelief and overwhelming emotion. Her lips trembled, but a genuine smile began to form, breaking through the years of pain and loneliness. For the first time in decades, she felt a warmth in her heart that melted away the cold.

She took a deep breath, and with a steady hand, she reached for the switch that would light up the Christmas tree. As she flipped it, the tree blazed to life, its lights casting a beautiful glow over the town square.

A wave of warmth seemed to spread through the crowd. One by one, people began to clap again, some wiping away tears of their own. Jack moved through the crowd, his eyes never leaving Evelyn's face, and when he reached her, he took her hand in his.

"You should have told me," he said quietly, his voice thick with emotion. "I would have understood. What your father did was never your fault, you were just a child. I still care for you, Evelyn. I always have."

Evelyn looked at him, her eyes filled with a mix of hope and disbelief. The crowd erupted into a cheer, and Sadie's heart swelled with happiness. For the first time, it seemed like Evelyn had a chance to let go of her past and embrace the love and acceptance she had always yearned for.

Chapter 12

A Town Christmas
to Remember

The night of Christmas Eve was a scene straight out
of a fairytale. The town square was filled once again
with twinkling lights, carol singers' joyous songs,
and the aroma of warm cider wafting through the
crisp winter air. The once dreary town had been
transformed into a vibrant celebration of
Christmas, thanks to the efforts of Sadie, Noel, and
the entire community.

Sadie walked through the square with Noel by her side, feeling a profound sense of accomplishment. The Christmas Fair had been a resounding success, and the town was alive with the spirit of the season. The joy and camaraderie that filled the air were palpable, and Sadie couldn't help but smile as she looked around at the happy faces of her new friends and neighbours.

Miss Jeffers, now Evelyn Roberts, had been welcomed into the heart of the town, her past pain replaced with the warmth of genuine affection. She had spent the past few days visiting various homes, enjoying the festive dinners and the love that had been extended to her. Each invitation was a testament to the change she had helped bring about in the town. Evelyn had finally found the family she had longed for all her life, and for the first time, she was looking forward to a warm, magical Christmas Day surrounded by love, laughter, and Jack's caring family.

As the evening drew to a close, Sadie found a quiet spot by the Christmas tree, its lights shimmering like a thousand tiny stars. She felt Noel's presence beside her, the small elf's mischievous grin brightening the night.

"Do you think they're happy?" Sadie asked, her voice filled with wonder.

Noel's eyes sparkled with mirth. "Oh, I'm sure they are. And you've done something truly special here, Sadie. You've shown everyone that the true spirit of Christmas is about love, kindness, and community spirit."

Sadie nodded, feeling a warmth in her heart that she hadn't felt since moving to this town. The holiday season had brought so much more than she had imagined. It had brought her new friends, a sense of belonging, and the joy of giving and receiving love.

As the clock struck midnight, the square was filled with the sound of laughter and the clinking of glasses as people celebrated the arrival of Christmas Day. The night sky was clear and filled with stars, a perfect backdrop to the festive scene below.

Noel looked at Sadie with a twinkle in his eye. "It's time for me to go," he said. "There are other children who need a bit of Christmas magic. But remember, Sadie, the magic of Christmas is not just in believing in Father Christmas. It's in believing in kindness, love, and the joy of giving."

Sadie hugged Noel tightly, feeling a pang of sadness at his departure. "Thank you for everything, Noel. You've helped make this Christmas truly magical." Noel gave her one last mischievous smile before disappearing into the night, his tiny feet leaving no trace as he went off to help others in need of holiday cheer.

As Sadie turned her gaze back to the town, she felt a deep sense of satisfaction. The Christmas Fair had brought the town together, and Evelyn had finally found the acceptance and warmth she had longed for. Sadie had learned that even though her family was busy, they loved her deeply, and that the magic of Christmas lay in the love and kindness they shared.

With a heart full of gratitude, Sadie went home to find her parents waiting for her with warm hugs and smiles. They spent the rest of the night together, sharing stories and laughter, and enjoying the festive spirit that had filled their home.

Later that night, Sadie sat down at her desk and picked up her pen. She wrote a final letter to Father Christmas, thanking him for sending Noel and helping her find a way to make this Christmas special for everyone, including herself. She set the letter in an envelope and placed it on 1. windowsill, feeling content and at peace.

As she climbed into bed, she thought about the past few weeks and the incredible journey she had been on. She knew that the magic of Christmas was not just in the gifts or the decorations, but in the love and kindness that people shared with one another. And that was a magic that would never fade, no matter how much time passed.

With a smile on her face, Sadie drifted off to sleep, her dreams filled with the warmth and joy of the Christmas season. The town had found its spirit once again, and in doing so, had shown that even the coldest hearts could be warmed by the kindness and love of others. It was a Christmas to remember, a testament to the power of hope, and the true magic of the holiday season.

Printed in Great Britain
by Amazon